Never Give Up

TERRI DUNN STAMPER

PAGE PUBLISHING, INC.
Conneaut Lake, PA

First originally published by Page Publishing 2020

ISBN 978-1-64628-963-9 (pbk)
ISBN 978-1-64701-772-9 (hc)
ISBN 978-1-64628-964-6 (digital)

Printed in the United States of America

Ollie is a playful otter; he loves to swim and play all day. One day, he was floating down the river when he heard someone crying. He looked around, and he saw a sad little turtle on the bank, crying.

He went up to the turtle and said, "Hello. My name is Ollie. What is your name?"

The little turtle wiped his eyes and said, "My name is Tate."

Ollie asked him, "Why are you crying?"

Tate replied, "I need to get to the other side of the river, and I can't swim. My family is on the other side, and I am sure they are very worried. We were taking a walk, and I got too close to the edge and fell in. They didn't know I fell. As I was floating down the river, there was a branch in the water, so I grabbed it and pulled myself up on the bank, but it's the wrong side." Tate started to cry again. He said, "I give up. I'll never get to my family."

Ollie said, "Please don't cry. I will help you get home, just don't give up!"

Tate dried his eyes and said, "Okay, we can try."

Ollie told Tate to take his shell off. "Maybe it's too heavy and that's why you sink?"

With Ollie's help, they got his shell off. Tate was at the edge of the water. Ollie said, "Okay. Are you ready?"

Tate said, "Here I go!"

He was in the water and thought he was swimming, but he wasn't swimming at all and started to sink. Ollie yelled, "Oh no!" He jumped in the water and pulled Tate by his tail to the bank.

Tate put his shell back on and started crying again. He told Ollie, "I give up. I'll never get to the other side!"

Ollie told him, "Never give up. We will try something different."

It was getting dark. Ollie told Tate, "We need to sleep, and we will start again in the morning." Ollie knew Tate was afraid, so he stayed with him all night. Poor little Tate. He cried himself to sleep.

The next morning, Ollie told Tate he saw some rocks above the water, down the bank. He told Tate, "You can walk across to the other side."

They got to the rocks, and Tate started walking across the rocks. He almost got to the other side, but there were no more rocks. There was too much water to get to the other side. Tate's legs were too short. He turned around and started back to Ollie.

Tate yelled, "I give up!"

Ollie told him, "Never give up!" Ollie had another idea. He told Tate to gather as many sticks as he can find. "We will build a bridge."

They stared building the bridge. They were almost done, just needed a few more sticks, but there were no more sticks. The bridge was too short!

Tate started crying very hard, and he asked Ollie, "Can I give up now?"

Ollie told him, "No. Never give up!"

They sat on the bank for a very long time. Thinking and thinking. All of a sudden, Ollie yelled, "I got it! I will get you to the other side this time!"

He was so excited, but Tate wasn't so sure since nothing has worked. He trusted his new friend, and he has tried very hard to help him get to the other side. Ollie told Tate to get on his back. "I will carry you on my back to the other side."

Tate said, "Oh no. I am too heavy. You will sink."

Ollie said, "I am very strong and a very good swimmer. I can do it because I never give up."

Tate climbed on Ollie's back, and he was very afraid. He closed his eyes and squeezed them tightly.

Ollie told him to hold tight. "Here we go!"

Ollie told Tate to open his eyes. "See. You are on the other side!"

Tate opened his eyes and was so surprised and happy to be on the other side. Ollie was very happy too.

Ollie told Tate, "Remember, never give up!"

They looked up, and at the top was Tate's worried family. They were so happy to see him.

Ollie jumped into the water and told Tate, "Remember, never give up."

They stayed friends for a very long time and had many adventures and made new friends. Tate still can't swim. He keeps trying because he remembers to never give up.

About the Author

Terri Dunn Stamper lives in Ohio with her husband. She has two sons, both are married. She read to her sons when they were young. She knows the impact reading has on a child, and this inspired her to write this book. Her book is about encouragement, friendship, and problem-solving. She hopes this book will encourage children to never give up and to help their friends when they have a problem.